<u>PRAI</u>

"Noonan's back catalog... pretty much humps the shit out of it."

—David Roth, *VICE*

"I adore Lacey Noonan's writing style."

—Leonard Delaney, *author of Conquered by Clippy*

"Lacey Noonan has truly catapulted herself, however knowingly, into the pantheons of greatest American authors (F. Scott Fitzgerald, Mark Twain, etc.), greatest female American authors (Willa Cather, Toni Morrison, etc.), and greatest humans (Jesus, Julius Caesar, etc.) to have ever set foot on this great Earth we call home."

—Brenden, *amazon reviewer*

"...one of the literary masters of our time..."

—Jonathan C. Pike, *amazon reviewer*

<u>PRAISE FOR *I DON'T CARE IF MY BEST FRIEND'S MOM IS A SASQUATCH, SHE'S HOT AND I'M TAKING A SHOWER WITH HER ...BECAUSE IT'S THE NEW MILLENNIUM*</u>

"It's somewhere between 'Ulysses' and 'iPad for Dummies'. Closer to the latter though."

—herbalt, *amazon reviewer*

"Anyhoodle, [this book is] frigging hilarious... From the copyright pirate warning, to the chapter headings, to line after line of really funny prose, this short is full of whip-sharp dialogue and clever turns of phrase."

—Acesfull, *amazon reviewer*

a

The Dishes Are Done Man!

book

BOOKS BY *Lacey Noonan*

NOVELLAS

A Cruzmas Carol: Ted Cruz Takes a Dickens of a Constitutional

Seduced by the Dad Bod: Book One in the Chill Dad Summer Heat Series

Hot Boxed: How I Found Love on Amazon

The Babysitter Only Rings Once

I Don't Care If My Best Friend's Mom is a Sasquatch, She's Hot and I'm Taking a Shower With Her …Because It's the New Millennium

I Don't Care if My Sasquatch Lover Says the World is Exploding, She's Hot But I Play Bass and There's Nothing Hotter Right Now Than Rap-Rock …Because It's the New Millenium (Book 2)

Eat Fresh: Flo, Jan and Wendy and the Five Dollar Footlong

A Gronking to Remember

A Gronking to Remember 2: Chad Goes Deep in the Neutral Zone

NOVELS

Shipwrecked on the Island of the She-Gods: A South Pacific Trans Sex Adventure

COLLECTIONS

The Hotness: Five Burning Hot Novellas

The Nasty Woman's Guide to Deplorable Baskets

The Blacker the Robot the Moister the Oyster

Falling for the Obamacare Sex Robot

My Obamacare Nightmare Book 2

LACEY NOONAN

ISBN: 154326316X
ISBN-13: 978-1543263169

Special Thanks

George Washington, Thomas Jefferson, James Madison, Benjamin Franklin, Thomas Paine and all you other big time ballers in scraggly wigs and tight pantaloons…

CONTENTS

To America

The Blacker the Robot the Moister the Oyster

The cistern contains: the fountain overflows.
—William Blake

Time to get wet, get wild, get wild, get wet.
—95 South

CHAPTER ONE

Suddenly Bethany

I awoke, happier than I'd awoken in a long time. The orgasm—*good Lord that orgasm!*—had freed me like Abraham Lincoln. I'd fallen asleep blubbering, the color of amber in my eyes, yellow and joyous. And sweet dreams had bathed me in their happy glows all night.

On dwindling waves of pleasure, I rode the Sea of Nod, until my sleep ship had touched the sandy bottom of morning.

Man, that doppelganger was a doozy of a fingerbanger. What other delights awaited me, I thought… but only fleetingly, for I dared not think of where this naughtiness headed.

I stretched and smiled. Even the bump had slept well inside me, nary a karate chop all night.

When you're pregnant, a good night's sleep is more precious than chocolate diamonds. I rolled over and was surprised to see the Obamacare Sex Robot sitting in a chair, still wearing my pink sweatsuit, staring straight ahead quietly. Strange. It would take some time to get used to that. Of course the machine didn't need to sleep, probably just reboot whenever Microsoft Excel crashed inside it or something.

The robot turned to me and smiled its not-quite-right, robotic smile, some kind of digital ropes and pulleys lifting the sides of its mouth and showing its porcelain teeth to me in accordance with the scene its optical sensors sensed and it algorithms' response to the environment. Weird. I forgot that it was weird. Which kind of bummed me out…

Oh my God, what the *hell* was I doing!

I sat up quickly in bed.

On the run from the law… from my husband, from my mother. And shacking up with an Obama thingie. An Obama! Guilt oozed in around the edges of my mind like black oil in the Gulf of Mexico. I started to feel low, so very low in the body and spirit.

But then a quiver of remembrance, a crotch

aftershock, shook my feminine fault line. And the feelings of the night before shimmied across my mind like a vase on a shelf. The memory came back whole-hog in one fell swoop: What happened the night before was pussy-joy pure and simple and good and goddamn if that ain't the cat's pajamas!

Wow, right?

The thoughts came fast and loose: Who cared if it was by a dumb Democrat robot? A woman's pussy is apolitical, I realized. Just beat the pussy up and you can count on *my* vote. (I don't think politicians, males especially, talk about pussies, vaginas, hoohas and women in general enough in the halls of power, tbh.) Shoot, it wasn't so bad, getting molested by a D-Crat—my body didn't know what rocked it, only that it had been rocked and rocked like a hurricane.

Still, I needed distraction. I wasn't used to having to think so much so early in the morning. "Turn on the TV or something, will you?" I said to Obama.

The TV was one of those old square shitboxes with fake brown wood on the side, sitting on a cart, facing the bed. The robot stood and turned a knob. The TV flicked on. I was surprised that it worked. And that it actually picked up CNN. The advertisement for "Free Cable" on the decrepit sign out front wasn't false advertising.

What was *on* CNN, however, was horrifying.

"—bring you now to Connecticut with breaking news. A local police officer has been attacked by Barack Obama. That's right, you heard right. By President Barack Obama himself."

I shot up in bed.

On the TV, to the left of the reporter, they played blurry footage on a loop. It was from a different angle than I'd experienced it, but it most certainly was footage from the day before. My traffic stop. It was the police officer's point of view. The naked Obamacare Sex Robot whisks around my SUV and hoists the cop in the air. A blur of green and white is all that is shown while the police officer flies through the air. He must have been wearing a body camera. "Beryl Furnette is on the scene. We go there now, live. Hi Beryl."

"Hi, Taffy."

"Any word on who the woman in the vehicle with President Obama is?"

"Not yet, Taffy. Authorities are staying mum.

Though we do know that assaulting a police officer is a felony and carries with it a mandatory minimum of a lifetime prison sentence. And kidnapping of the president, which is treason, carries with it another five hundred hours of community service."

"This is insane," I said to the robot. "Why don't they confirm with the actual president that you're not the actual president! This is nuts! Typical fucking CNN drumming up fervor without due diligence! A bitching birch tree has more journalistic integrity than liberal-ass media CNN! Fuck!"

And then there it was: my face on the TV. A freeze frame of me sitting in my SUV, while I was talking to the police officer. Anyone who knew me would recognize me instantly from the photo. It was only a matter of time before the police found out. Maybe they already knew. Maybe they were already on the way here. I'd used my credit card to book the room last night like a stupid idiot. Stupid, stupid, stupid! Idiot! Idiot! Idiot! Credit Card! Credit Card! Credit Card!

"Taffy, police are trying to track down the identity of this woman. They are not sure how she managed to kidnap and brainwash the president into protecting her, but there it is."

"Mainstream media!" I screamed. "What the shit is this???????"

Suddenly…

Yes, so very *suddenly*…

There was a knock at the door. I screamed with fright and pulled the covers up to my chin.

"Would you like me to answer the door, Holly?" the Obamacare *Bx-44* Sex Robot asked.

"No!" I hissed. "And lower your voice."

"Would you like me to answer the door, Holly?" the robot said again at the same exact, infuriating volume, only in a deeper register, like Barry White.

The person knocked again. Louder this time.

"What do we do what do we do?" I said.

"Answer a door that is knocked upon?" the robot ventured.

"Are you crazy?"

"I am a robot. I am neither sane nor insane. I merely perform preordained functions, primarily in the industries of adult hospitality, but also self-defense and midwifery and husbandry."

"What if it's the police here to arrest us? I can't been seen with an Obamacare Sex Robot! Especially one that *looks* like Obama! I can't!

Obama's a Socialist Nazi-Crat Demtard! We have to get out somehow."

"Who is this 'Obama' you keep mentioning?" The Obamacare Sex Robot asked. "Is it some kind of Gaelic mispronunciation of our nation's twenty-second state, Alabama?"

"What? You don't know who Barack Obama is? What the hell? *How?*"

The door knocked again.

"Oh God, oh God, oh God. Okay. Creep to the door and see who it is through the peephole."

But before Obama could sneak like a creep to the peep, I heard Bethany's voice. "Holly!" she whisper-yelled, "Holly! Are you in there? It's me, Beth!" She rapped again on the door.

How the fuck did Bethany find us? My dumb drunk mom-friend Bethany. This was crazy. Not just crazy, but like cray-cray level crazy. Did Brad-Brad squeal on me or had she already seen the news this morning? Bethany wasn't exactly Miss Up-To-Date on the latest goings on. Whatever news managed to slink through the cracks in *US Weekly* like a slinky dress on Kate Moss was all she knew about… Kardashian-Stefani-Anniston this and that.

"Should I answer the door now, Holly?"

Obama asked.

"No! Ssh!" I whispered at him. Jeez, this hard-on machine had a real hard-on for opening doors all of a sudden.

The robot froze midstride.

A few moments passed, more pregnant than my fat ass.

Silence, scary cray-cray silence.

Finally, I heard Bethany walk away. A minute later she was knocking on the door next over. I heard a person mumble inside the room, cough up a menthol-ravaged lung a bunch, then answer the door. Within seconds there was shouting, screaming, scuffling. It sounded like low-class chaos.

This was my chance!

"Come on, Obama!" I shouted.

I heaved myself from the bed, threw on my shoes, pulled up my panties and shimmied my dress down over my hips.

The scuffle next door seemed to intensify. Whatever was happening out there, Bethany would surely be occupied by it.

I squinted through the peephole. Couldn't see anything. I snatched my fob from the dresser and unlocked the SUV parked in front of the room while we were still inside. I looked through the peephole again…

The coast was clear.

"Let's go!" I yelled.

The door flung open and me and the sex robot bolted for the car!

Chapter Two
Bx-44 Love-WD-44

This story is a story of impressions. Large and small. It's a story of great and sweeping history, of preconceived notions battling in the skies like Norse gods, yes, but it's also a story of small, personal moments, so brief in existence, but lasting forever in the mind, as if a great artist had captured them in oils, like Michelangelo or van Gogh, hanging now in great museums across the world, delighting dreamers, inspiring poets, photographed by Japanese tourists. I suppose I can stretch the analogy further, using Impressionism or Post-Impressionism as a launch pad to add expressive dabs of personal color like Van Gogh or Matisse, but I think it behooves me to get to the story—to the impression that will forever be frozen in my memory of the vignette I witnessed as I hurried into my SUV like a madwoman outside of this Wayward Inn in Bumfucksborough, Connecticut.

I trundled up behind the wheel of the Lexus SUV, huffing, oofing and grunting.

"Jesus, you're fast!" I said, starting the car, revving the engine. The Obamacare Sex Robot was already buckled up in the passenger seat next to me, placid face looking forward, ever the fashion plate in my pink sweats, its massive dark cock tenting the front of the pants.

What the robot's reply was, if he did in fact reply, I don't remember. Because what I saw erased all other sense perception…

On the sidewalk, just to the left of the hood of the car, Bethany, and someone I could only describe as a very tall albino man with a small black nose wearing a white fur coat and even white fur pants—like a seven foot tall pimp— were beating the living shit out of a screaming hillbilly hobo.

My jaw hit the floor mat.

Bethany's albino pimp had the hobo in a headlock and was shaking him back and forth like a dog trying to break a chew toy's neck, and all the while Bethany—my mom-friend Bethany, mother of Aiden, Jayden and Rayden—laid into the guy's face with devastating blow after blow, her fists leaving knuckle-marks on his cheeks, chin and forehead. What little teeth the man had to begin with flew away in the wind like confetti. It was all so confusing yet visually stimulating.

But then the hobo pulled a gun from out of his soiled pants.

Reality squeezed my lungs… I nearly fainted. *What if a bullet hit me?* I began to panic. Bethany, WTF! Then I saw it was maybe a tazer of some kind—but that didn't matter now because Bethany ripped it right out of his hands and started beating the hobo in the face with it. All three were screaming, fuming like contestants on the *Price is Right*. Utter chaos.

"Where are they!?" Bethany screamed into the motel-curmudgeon's battered face.

He spat teeth and blood at her. "Fuck you, rich bitch!"

Bethany smacked him across the face so hard I felt it in the car. "Where is she!? Where is he!? Where are Holly and Obama!?" she screamed.

I snapped out of it. So they *were* after us.

My jaw clenched. Whatever the hell this brouhaha was, I wanted *no* part of it. I put the

SUV in reverse and slammed on the gas. I certainly do not put the *bro* in brouhaha or even *haha*. No. Uh-uh.

The SUV screamed and I laid rubber backwards on the pavement like a dog scuttling his poopy butt on the ground.

Bethany spun around. So did her pimp-compatriot-in-felony-assault. They recognized me instantly.

I slammed on the brakes and turned the steering wheel; it was that sensitive moment in a three point turn when you're a sitting duck...

"Holly!" Bethany screamed.

I put the SUV in drive.

Bethany dropped the curmudgeon like a sack of Irish potatoes onto the sidewalk next to the furry white man and bolted after the car, waving the tazer at us like an A1 psycho. "Holly, wait! I just want to... like, talk to you for a sec!" she yelled, her arms waving, eyes glaring, teeth baring, blood on her knuckles. She looked like a Rocky Balboa Medusa. "Wait up, bitch, wait up!"

"Holy fuck!" I screamed, my nerves electric.

I slammed on the gas. Our backs pressed against the seat as if we were taking off in the Space Shuttle. Bethany reached the car just as we lurched away. Her hands pounded on the passenger side window, leaving a streak of blood on the glass.

Seconds later we were careening down the road. I took the first left in the green woods and then kept taking them. If Bethany and that dude came after us again I wasn't going to make it so easy for them.

But how did she find us in the first place? I thought. Was it dumb luck? We were at least thirty, forty, fifty miles from our town. My female brain was getting wacked in the face in the glass racquetball court of my mind again.

"It is time for *change*," The Obama next to me intoned, breaking my train of thought.

I popped from my reverie. "*What?* Not *now*, Obama Llama Ding Dong. No politics, *please*. Not now. Not ever."

"Apologies. Might I recommend a change *of vehicle*?" it said.

"Huh?"

"There will be many authorities after us now, of numerous agencies: local, state, federal, Bethany. They will be looking for a vehicle of this exact description."

"How the fuck am I supposed to get a new

car, Obama? You want me to swing by the Lexus dealership and sign on the bottom line for a new one? That takes hours. The loan. The credit check. Assessing the trade-in value, of which, well, this car has *very little* now with the smashed-in back, the blood streaks and Jesus what the heck am I *talking* about this is all so crazy cray-cray double cray!"

I began to cry. The tears came wet and warm from my eyes like a hot August rain.

Where was I supposed to go? I had the powerful urge to call hubby Bradley again, that fucking moron. He did this. He did *all* this. Did he ever love me? What did I do to deserve such a backstabbing, closeted homosexual idiot for a husband, who at the first sight of a self-lubricating penis was willing to throw away his entire history as a potent white male and join the crybaby liberal army pansies, the CLAP? Why hadn't I seen it before? Why had I been so blind to the obvious truth? A lineup of old college boyfriends and party flings suddenly presented themselves in my head, possible replacements for the monster I had married if the incredible lightness of being hadn't been so incredible or so light. They were tall, short, skinny, fat, smart dumb, but they were all straight-up, straight American men. Then I envisioned Bradley. Us, courting, younger. At the club. At the marina. Out on Bradley's dad's sailboat. Making love. Marrying. Pregnant! Oh, God! The father of my child did this to me!

"Bradley!" I cried. Tears exploded from my eyes again. The road blurred. My hands weakened on the steering wheel. The SUV swerved towards a tree.

The cyborg's hand grabbed the wheel. My feet came off the gas and the car slowed to a stop by the side of the road. I dissolved into sad moisture like an Alka-Seltzer.

The robot opened his door and jumped out, but I barely took notice. I didn't care. I hoped it ran away. All the way back to the White House for all I cared—sign some NAFTA-rific legislation or something. I rested my head on the steering wheel and used my First Amendment Rights to cry. Like a town crier, I cried. I really let it out.

Seconds later a car pulled up. It honked. I looked up, fully expecting to see Bethany or the police, but it was the Obamacare Sex Robot. The car was a small red Datsun, and the robot was behind the steering wheel smiling at me.

"Hop in, ma'am, please," Obama said.

I sighed and got into the Datsun, resigning resignedly my fate to the Fates, leaving the SUV running where it stood on the side of the road. We drove off.

A few minutes later, the Pleasure Bot spoke: "I chose a red vehicle as it represents the Republican Party, your voter-registered form of government," Obama said. "Do you like it? To where shall we drive? Would you like a perineal massage?"

"No."

"But what about—" The Obamacare Sex Robot cut himself off. It suddenly hummed, beeping and clanking—something important was happening inside him—and it grabbed by the hair and yanked me down towards its crotch.

I screamed. The robot was going to force me to suck its dick! Finally, this evil robot was showing its true colors!

"Hey!" I yelled, "Ew! NO! NO!"

I fought against it as much as possible but the robot had an iron grip. My face was pressed against its groin. My face was mashed into my very own pink sweatpants, and against something absolutely *rock hard* underneath it, which now began to gyrate very slowly. I screamed again and then pressed my lips together. No way in hell was I going to get a mouthful of this robot's love-WD-40!

"Mrs. McQuerty, please refrain from squirming. There is an armored police vehicle approaching in the oncoming lane."

"What?"

"Four hundred meters and closing."

"Oh, Jesus."

"Steady. Steady. It appears the vehicle does not register us. Surely the vehicle is searching for a silver SUV with black leather interior and significant rear-end damage. Two hundred meters."

"Of course an Obama robot would use meters. Typical Eurofag élite," I said and turned my head, resting my cheek on the president's mechanical dick. It wasn't so bad this way. Did I actually enjoy being this close to it? What was it like to, well…

"One hundred… *yards*. Fifty. Zero yards."

A whooshing of air rattled the Datsun. A shadow crossed over us. In my peripheral vision I saw a blur of a huge truck pass us. It was camouflaged and looked mean—something that should have been running over terrorists' mud huts in Afghanistan, not patrolling the wooded lanes and dappled roads of American Connecticut.

The *Bx-44* released its iron grip on my head and I sat upright, breathing heavy.

"I'm afraid it will not be long before the authorities locate us."

I panicked. "We need to escape! Canada! Let's go to Canada!"

"Negative. My program will not allow me to leave the borders of this nation. Is there a safe place of which you are cognizant, a place where no authority would think to look for you?"

"I have no idea!" I cried.

I leaned my face against the window and watched the trees blur past, bereft, the world closing in, nowhere to run, nowhere to hide. What was the point of anything, I thought. Eventually the darkness will find you. What's the point of fighting? Life is just this little bright blip of constant surrender and capitulation to the storm of forces already in motion the day you're born. Maybe if you're lucky you can sneak in some fun, some out-of-bounds joy, the type of joy you always thought possible when you were a kid when your parents weren't looking—the type of joy parents always seemed to withhold... If only they bothered! They'd have so much fun, with their power and freedom of choice. It was just *right there* for the taking. Why did they never bother to have fun, our parents with their homes and cars and pools and money...

Then it hit me.

All this sneaking around and skullduggery or whatever you call it was starting to have an impact on me. I could hang. I could manage in the Skullduggery Department. I thought of a good place to hide.

"Wait! No, wait! I *do* have an idea!" I sat upright and shouted.

CHAPTER THREE
High-Risk Pool

We ditched the Datsun, hid it under a blanket of branches and leaves, and walked the rest of the way through the woods. The Obamacare Sex Robot threw his arm around my waist and helped me over the rockier parts where I was unsteady with my frontload. He held my hand the rest of the way. We were like Hansel and Gretel. By the time we finally got inside I was exhausted, tired and sweaty. My enfattened Gretel thighs were chafed to high holy heaven.

"I really need a bath," I said, easing myself onto the bed upstairs.

"I will run the faucet," the tireless Robot replied.

The droid disappeared into the adjoining bathroom, I heard a metallic squeak and then the enchanting sound of water splashing on porcelain.

I sat up and kicked my shoes off and looked around the room. It had been years since I'd seen it, but nothing had changed. The second-to-most-expensive wallpaper, the tasteful yet not-that-tasteful Walnut and Beechwood colonial dresser, bed and chairs—it was all so very nice-looking, though the question lingered in your mind: was all this fake or from a thrift store? The room was so decidedly, nearly commonplacely elegant, which was my mother's way of letting friends and family know that she thought lower of them. For this was the guest house behind my mother's house, and if a guest was relegated to the guest house out past the pool, it was a statement: *You are shit, my love.* And more importantly: no one ever stayed here or came out here anymore. My mother's alienating tendencies had seen to that. My parents had divorced years ago and dad lived in Helsinki or Davos or Uruguay or someplace like that. So it was the perfect hideout. Also, as a bonus, it was around noon, and I knew my mother would be at the club. She'd be there all day, brunching like the Queen Bee (B for Bitch) she was. So we were safe here for the time being.

"The bath is ready, Mrs. McQuerty," The Obamacare Sex Robot said, strolling into the bedroom, like the Commander-in-Chief casually strolling down the red carpet in Cross Hall in the White House to speak to the press with his big ears and pink track suit.

"Please don't call me that. At least not right now. I want nothing to do with the McQuerty clan at present, please and thank you, Barack *Hussein* Nobama."

"The bath is ready… Mrs.… Sexy Lady."

"Ahh, that's better."

And the robot bowed, with a tender, meaningful smile on its lips, like a butler in hot pink livery. I looked and saw steam coming from the bathroom.

"Tell you what," I said. "I'm boiling from that walk through the woods. Let's hit the pool instead. Come on." I lumbered up from the (insulting) bed.

"Is that wise?"

"To cool off? Hells yes."

"Will we be seen?"

"Jeez, don't be a pussy. I thought you weren't supposed to know who Barack Obama was? You're certainly acting like him right now."

We went down the spiral stairs in the front of the guest house to the pool area. It was in the backyard and hidden from the road, surrounded by thick woods on the sides, except where the expansive side lawn went to meet the six car garage. The nearest neighbors were hundreds of yards away, over the river and through the woods, out of sight.

The blue water called my name (Mrs. Sexy Lady).

I stripped down to my oversized preggo bra and panties and slid into the shallow end. The water was cool and instantly refreshing. I ducked down under the surface, mottled with sunlight that sluiced through the leaves overhead, and floated there a while, holding my breath, feeling at one with the little amniotic fish in my belly. When colored lights started appearing in my eyes from lack of oxygen I surfaced again—head tilted back, long light brown hair stuck wetly to my head, like sexpots do in the movies.

Pools always made me feel good. All the crazy negativity, all the confusion and horror of the past two days drifted away. *Things could work here*, I thought. Just live in the pool house for a while, slum it with the second-rate furniture and my robot sex-butler, my sweet president in our presidential suite. No one would ever know or think to look here.

And I was actually starting to feel there floating in the refreshing pool something like *happy*. "I," I said to myself, "didn't realize how much I'd needed this—Oh!—Um, hello?" The Obamacare Sex Robot was directly in front of me in the deep end of the pool, still in my pink workout clothes, treading water and looking at me with that calculating cyborgesque look in his eyes. "Are you...? Um. *What* are you doing?"

"A swimming pool offers a wonderful opportunity for expectant mothers to stretch and exercise."

"Okay."

"May I?"

"May you what?"

"This." The aqua-POTUS-bot paddled over to me. I watched with wariness as he swam around my backside.

"You're not going to drown me because I'm Republican are you?" I said, suddenly nervous that I was alone in a pool with an African-American (sorry, force of habit) robot that occasionally did such strange and surprising things. How could I be sure this droid really had my best interests programmed in his stupid hard drive or whatever? I looked around the pool and there seemed suddenly to be an ocean of water in every direction, the edges miles away. It was risky what I was doing. I was in a High-Risk Pool, where the chances of drowning were so much higher because of who I was and what had been done to me (copulation with an eye to accouchement) but what did it matter at this point—no one could save me and my pre-existing condition except myself and if that ain't American-USA-Butt-Blasting-Constitutional-Freedom I don't know what is.

"That is *highly* against my protocol," Obama replied and placed his hands on my hips. He pushed me forward and we tugboated towards the deep end.

"What do you have in mind?" I said, starting to feel a little nervous, perhaps because I was also, against my better wishes, starting to feel a little *something else*. The robot's firm hands on my hips reminded me again of the massage in the motel the night before—the amber and yellow globs of blobbing ecstasy.

The birds chirped in the trees all around us,

and the bees buzzed on the flowers hedging the yard.

"Water fitness offers high-resistance to opposite muscle groups simultaneously, while the buoyancy prevents overloading of joints and tendons."

"Oh," I said.

We were in the deep end now. I began to paddle and kick but it wasn't good enough. With my extra weight I started to sink. Water was suddenly at my neck. I grunted. The robot released my hips and placed his hands under my ass. He lifted me up and in a second we made it to the other end of the pool. I grabbed hold of the side and, hufflepuffing and puffalumping, held myself there, marooned on the side of the pool like a beached whale.

Without a moment's pause, the Obamacare Gratification System went underwater behind me and then went to town.

Did the Obamacare Sex Robot know what I wanted before I knew I wanted it?

With that, the robot pulled off my underpants underwater, dragged them right down off my ass and down my legs. I looked out the corner of my eye and saw them float away like a jellyfish in the pool. Then with utmost skill he unlatched my brassiere and it fell off my chest into the water. My two boobs, twice as big as normal, plopped into the water.

Suddenly: I was skinny-dipping.

"Oh, why not?" I giggled. It felt naughty and fun and young. I kicked my legs and felt the milky water on my body. *All the times I've been in this pool and it's the first time I've ever done this*, I thought.

But then the thinking ended. The Obamacare Robot touched me. His finger flicked me off like a light switch: I closed my eyes, let the cool water and air relax me and the sun's rays heal me.

Down below the surface of the water the pleasure robot began to massage my ass. I could feel his legs pumping to keep himself afloat, and that added to the pleasure—the water caressing around my body like jets in a hot tub.

I shuddered.

The robot palmed each cheek, taking my jiggly meat in each hand, squeezing, kneading. Swirls of pleasure whirled up into my body. I began to breathe faster. My heart began to thump in my chest. Under the water I spread my legs and the dirty Democrat robot began to stroke the cleft between my ass, running his thumb up and down the fertile valley between my cheeks. Then he reached his hands under me and began stroking up around the front of my body, just below my bump and then back up around to my ass. Long stroke after long stroke after long, slow stroke…

"Yes," I whispered and exhaled.

"*Like* that?" the robot asked.

"Oh yessss," I drawled, then: "Can you keep yourself up in the water?"

"It is not difficult for me. Also, I do not have to keep myself above the water for I do not breathe oxygen," he said, and palmed my pussy.

Whoa.

I lost my grip on the side of the pool and fell, my nipples sliding along the rough tile, which percolated unexpected pins and needles of delight throughout my body.

But it was not as unexpected or as delightful as Obama's rock hard body pressing against my back to keep me up on the wall. Two dark arms were suddenly on either side of me. Underneath the surface of the water, between my legs, I felt my clam enwettify wetter than the water itself— my brackish mussel engorging in its native watery habitat as the dark robot enveloped me in pleasure. It's true. The saying was true: "The blacker the robot, the moister the oyster." His iron-hard chest pressed against my back. I was sandwiched between the president and the side of the pool, squished between two very, very, very hard things. I was a living, lady durometer.

The hardest thing, though, was the robot's... well, suddenly *it* was there, pressed against my ass, laying like an iron rod between my two velvety cheeks.

I exhaled hotly. "Oh God. Is that your..." I moaned.

Wordlessly, the Obama robot began grinding his hips into my rump. I hoisted myself up a little, presenting my ass to him. He grinded harder. I could feel my inner walls pulsating, myself opening up, the cool air on my back, goosebumps on my neck. I spread my legs and the robot slunk down into the water.

A second later I saw my pink gym clothes floating away in the pool.

"What are you going to do?" I asked nervously, biting my lower lip.

And then I felt it.

The head of the Barack Obama's metal cock pressed between my legs, like an exercise ball pressed against the mouth of my wishing well. "W-what are you going to do?" I asked again. I couldn't believe this was happening, but it was the only thing I wanted to happen in the whole world.

"What I was built for."

"Is it okay, I mean, that I'm pregnant?"

"It is more than okay. It is beneficial."

"I knew it!" I said, thinking of Brad-Brad's wimpy, sissy excuses. "You won't hurt me?"

"No. Well, maybe a *little*. Your sweet little hole is so tight," his robot voice unspooled in humanoid sex-speak.

"Oh God…"

Obama circled the hard tip of his dick around the lips of my pussy. I quivered with desire. I couldn't see it, but I could feel that Obama was *hung*. Most importantly though: he wanted me. Fucking needle-dick Bradley was too scared to even look at me naked when I was pregnant—the most beautiful I will ever be. And now the President of the United States or close enough was about to enter me. He was the law and it was the law and the law was never so virtuous.

Suddenly, thinking of needle-dick Bradley, a guilt grew inside me—if not yet the president's

Member of Congress. Could I cheat on my husband? I mean, I had Bradley by the short and curlies. When it came time for the Big D (Divorce not Dick), I could say in court what I witnessed in our bedroom yesterday without fear of reprisal: Bradley had cheated on me by getting it up the rear from *my* robot, and meanwhile I was a perfect, monogamous, doe-eyed angel.

But now…

"I—I'm not sure if you… that is, ooh, that feels amazing… But maybe we should wait, I don't know… ooh, man oh man…"

"Affirmative."

"Wait, what?"

Before I knew what happened, Obama slid down my backside under the water. Without another word the robot slinked beneath the surface like some creepy swamp creature.

But it was only me that was getting swampy.

Because Obama had a magic robot tongue.

Oh my God.

It started slow, a tickle here, a tab of the tongue there. First it was little butterfly kisses along the flowery folds of my womanhood.

Creepers of joy tap-danced up my spine, made my backside tingle.

My body awoke, a rhapsody of awakening that I wanted more of the more I felt it. I clutched at it, desperate for it. It was a need always achieving and always needing. And then the *Bx-44 Gratification System* increased the torment.

It was like the dirt motel all over again except up in a clear, affluent, watery heaven.

Down below the surface, the president held my hips fast and licked my pussy like a beast, his dark tongue darting into my dark hole there in the pool like an underwater cave. Plain and simple, he was burglarizing my Watergate. He took my folds into his mouth like a hired goon pilfering manila folders from a filing cabinet, then sucked me up and down, tap dancing his tongue across my lips like Woodward and Bernstein tapping out incendiary investigative journalism on a Smith-Corona typewriter.

I held onto the side of the pool for dear life.

I was like a drowning woman.

I laughed, I cried, I moaned.

I was coming. Oh my God I was coming. Well…

I was *about to* come, anyway…

"Holly!? Is that you!? What the hell are you doing down there!?" a voice rang out over the backyard and pool.

I screamed—crushed my two legs together on Barack's head with a frightened pressure that would have killed him if his head wasn't titanium-grade.

Where was the voice coming from? Who was it?

Of course.

Up on the balcony of the main house that overlooked the pool, white-knuckling the rail, very much not getting soused on Wine Spritzers at the club, staring down at me with supreme aghastness—The Aghastiocity of Hope—was Mumsy. It was my mother.

CHAPTER FOUR

Most Whores Aren't

Under the water I felt Obama abandon my nether regions like he'd abandoned the Middle Class. *Oh my God*, I thought, *what if my mother sees him!*

I let go of the side of the pool and tried to keep the president hidden underwater like a subprime mortgage. Jesus Christ, this was all I needed now. I kicked and pressed my hands down on his shoulders. I was so dang ungainly though, a fat pregnant whale, I splashed around like a big fat fish out of water in the water. And I went under.

"Help!" I screamed, splashing my arms, knowing full-well my mother would rather watch her only daughter drown than share a pool with a black person. "Haaalp!"

But then Obama surfaced. He grabbed hold

of me under my armpits and held me afloat. We motorboated slowly to the side of the pool.

"Holly, what the hell... are you naked?" my mother yelled. "Oh my God... and is that... Is that who *I think it is?* Oh, Holly, *really.* Our pool hasn't had a Democrat in it since those West Hartford kids broke in and scratched it to bloody hell with their skateboards that one winter."

"What are you doing home!" I screamed from the pool. "Why aren't you at the club getting hammered on—?" I struggled to get out of the robot's clutch. "Let me go! Let me go, will you?" I yelled, but then whispered to him: "My underwear, Robo-Bama, now!"

"Honestly, Holly. You asking *me* what *I'm* doing. You asking me what *I'm* doing in my own home, while you cavort about with that... that... *person* like a stupid little teenager. The Fox News was right. And Bradley. Ooh, know what? I'm going to go *call* him right now to come *pick* you up."

She turned to go inside, but a person blocked her way, stepping out from the sliding glass doors into the light. Not just a person—a strapping young lad. He was lean and muscular, tan with jet-black hair. The lad was handsome in an oily variety bohunk kind of way—a caddy of Italian extraction named Tony who I recognized from the club, always schmoozing with the older ladies. The whispers on the wind said he was a gigolo, a Good Time Johnny, but I never believed it. Until now, that is. Because, suffice it to say, Tony was buck-freaking-naked, his olive Mediterranean skin greased up and shiny, shiny cock and balls a-swingin'-in-the-breeze under a black tuft of pubic hair.

"And who the frig is that!?" I shouted from the pool (knowing full well who it was).

"It's, it's…" my mother stuttered. "Aye!" She screamed. "Help! A burglar! Help! Someone!" It was a terrible impression of a scared person. "Out! Out, vagrant! Shoo! Shoo!" She quickly ushered Tony back into the house, admonishing his chiseled butt with motherly spankings and slappings and then disappeared behind him.

Fifteen minutes later the four of us sat arguing on the lanai off the pool area. From its dappled shade, the lanai overlooked the expanse of lawn—a white gazebo out in the middle of it like a lone chess piece, and the green kingdom of

Connecticut beyond. I wore a big flowy, flowery maternity dress my mother had stashed away from her days as a progenitor. She didn't have a bra that fit me. My heavy boobs swung low like sweet chariots. Tony wore a sleeveless orange t-shirt and black jeans. My Obamacare Sex Machine sported business casual: tan slacks and a light blue button-down shirt abandoned by my father when he hightailed it out of our lives.

"How *dare* you bring this *thing* into my house!" my mother said, very much keyed-up.

"There was nowhere else for me to go, mother!"

"How about the post office to return it? The whole countryside is out with pitchforks looking for you, the police, the army, the navy, the coast guard, and here you are canoodling around in our pool like Brooke Shields and Christopher Atkins in *The Blue Lagoon*."

"I'm pregnant—with *your* grandchild—and I was *hot*. I swam to cool off, so sue me. Where else was I supposed to go swimming? Where else was I supposed to go?"

"I'm sorry, but there's always somewhere else to go when you're a *whore*, and that's to jail."

My jaw hit the lanai like a coconut falling

from a tree.

I stared at my mother, then looked from her to her oily bohunk, sitting in a chair quietly and nervously listening to us, then back to her. I raised my hand and pointed at Tony, like, *Hello!?*

"But I'm not married anymore!" my mother exclaimed.

"Most whores aren't."

Now it was my mother's turn to clean the tile with her chin. But rather than have the afternoon turn nastier than a twenty-day-old tampon, I tried to take it down a notch, "I didn't want anyone seeing me with him, that's all, mother. I know we have a reputation to uphold in this community."

"Well, that's the *first* sensible thing you've said *all* day. Possibly your whole life."

I paused, breathed deeply a bunch and counted to ten. This would take some art. "After what happened with Bradley, I panicked. Bradley was *so* scary all of a sudden, mommy, I was so scared. I just grabbed the robot and ran. You should have seen the look in his eyes, mother. Suddenly just so… *scary* and so… *homosexual*."

My mother raised her face and stabbed a mean, knife-like laugh into the vines on the lattice above us. Then she lowered a sardonic-as-fuck gaze at me, like I was still a wild child or something, disappointing.

"What the hell! It's the truth!" I yelled. I began breathing fast. Obama put his hand on my knee and I felt slightly calmer. My mother saw this and smirked. But then a look of serious surprise came over her.

"Wait, you haven't seen the news, have you?"

"The police thing on CNN? Yeah, I saw that. A bunch of typical liberal muckraking B.S. and lies, mother."

"What? No, not that." My mother stifled a sniffle. All of a sudden it looked like she was about to cry.

"Gayle..." tan Tony said softly, rising from his chair, cupping his crotch.

"It was just *so awful*, Holly! It was on in the parlor at the club. *All* the women, those catty *bitches*, those catty *cunts*, were looking at *me* and whispering to themselves.

"What was on?"

"And then when I tried to find a seat... no one would tip their hat to me. No one would let me sit with them. All the seats, taken. I know it was that seething bag of flesh Barbara Montaigne, it was her telling everyone I was a secret liberal.

Oh, Holly, I was so bereft, *so* insulted… and then Tony came and took me by the hand… and of course he's been so good to me, so *accommodating…*"

"What was on?"

"We decided to come back to my place and… Well… don't look at me like that, Holly, it's happened *many* times before and God willing it will happen many times again! He knows how to work the sides and up the middle—when to go hard as a board, when to pull back and go soft as a feather, because Tony's a *lover*, let me tell you. A *real* lover who knows how to please a woman! You think just because I'm older than you that I don't have needs? That I'm not still a woman with womanly needs, up to and including the slimy clutch of a greasy Italian boy? Well, screw you and the horse you rode in on, missy!"

"What was—?"

My mother flicked on the TV. (Yes, an outdoor TV, part of the outdoor entertainment system, where, apparently, she entertained Tony, who worked the sides and the middle in greasy fashion.) She clicked over to the local news.

In a flash, Bradley's face was on the screen. I gasped. He was standing in front of our house, in the driveway in fact, next to his busted car, speaking to reporters, a bouquet of microphones in front of his ugly mug.

"—think I feel bad, knowing it's still out there, still dangerous, dangerous to all law-abiding citizens. My name is Bradley McQuerty, entrepreneur, and I caught my wife with a sex robot—*sniff*—I mean, that's what they're for and I accept that as a registered Demtar—Democrat, but I was confused by what I saw, did not know what was going on, didn't know and couldn't have known she'd ordered a *pleasure bot*, thought she was being assaulted by a bla—by a *male*, um, person, and tried to protect her. But then the robot attacked me and the two ran off together. Holly, if you're hearing this, please, please, come home honey. And bring the robot. It's a felony to assault a police officer, to resist arrest, and to steal government property. Come on, honey, come on home. Your husband loves you. You're only making it worse by not coming forward."

"Liar!" I screamed at the TV.

Under Bradley's televised, dipshit face it said: *Former Strawberry Farm Owner.*

My mother sighed. On the TV the news channel started looping the scene with the cop yesterday.

"Tell her! Tell her what happened!" I said to the Obamacare Sex Robot.

"Holly and I had sexual relations in a hotel last night, Holly's mother. And in the pool we were just about—"

My mother gasped.

"NO! Not that! *Earlier!* With Bradley!"

"Bradley and I had sexual relations, anal intercourse, to be specific, in the McQuerty bedroom, what one might consider homosexual relations, which is legal in a good percentage of these United States of America, including—checking... checking...—the state of Connecticut. In addition to acting as the penetrating partner, I also offered a reach-around and we performed mutual oral sex as well, something colloquially known as—checking... checking...—the numeral sixty-nine."

"I walked in and Bradley was getting it up the *ass* from this here Sex Robot, mom! *That's* what was happening. That's why I freaked out and stole the robot. Can't you see now, can't you see now why you need to protect me and not be mad at me!"

My mother covered her ears. "No, no, no! I

don't believe it. It's *not natural*—intercourse with plastic and metal, no, no, no! Especially one that looks like a famous movie star. It's not right! Sex with a copy of someone who exists, who's won an Academy Award for Pete's sake!"

"But, Gayle…" Tony trailed off.

"Mother," I said, quieter, my mind stumbling upon the moss-covered clearing of a delightful confusion, "Who do you think this is again?" I asked, pointing to Obama.

"Oh, *you* know," she said, frowning, nodding knowingly.

"I know *I* know, but do *you* know?"

My mother looked at The Obamacare Sex Robot who was the spitting image of the sitting president sitting next to me, then to her boy toy, who opened his mouth to speak but held his Italian viper tongue, and then back to me.

Finally, she ventured, "Denzel Washington?"

"Ha!" I bounced up and down in my seat, laughing. "Ha! Ha! Ha!"

The robot did the same. "Ha! Ha! Ha!" it laughed, hopping in his chair, which naturally made me stop, but the hilarity was still chillin' in the lanai.

"Mom, it's Barack Obama! It's supposed to

look like the president!"

"What? They think the *president* assaulted a police officer in that video they keep showing? Is that why there is half an infantry division out looking for you? Did the liberal press stop to think to ask the White House if the president was kidnapped? This makes no sense whatsoever!"

"I have no idea!"

"Oh honey, I'm so sorry!" my mother said and threw her arms out wide. Her eyes were moist with tears. "Oh, Holly, mommy believes you. She believes you!" She hugged me and gripped me tight.

I squeezed her back. It felt good to be held by a human. By a mother. By my human mother. But in the middle of the reunion I became aware of a foreign sound intermingling with the bucolic sounds of campestral Connecticut.

My ears perked up. Engines? There was the sound of many diesel engines coming up the driveway at us. Driving fast. Were they police? Those scary cray-cray armored vehicles we saw patrolling the road?

"Mommy?" I said. She was squeezing me extra tight. She wouldn't let me go. The sounds of the engines got louder.

The pleasure cyborg got up and made a move to extract me from my mother's grip.

"Hands off, Denzel! I'm hugging my daughter!" she said. "This is a moment."

Suddenly, five speeding trucks barreled out onto the lawn: three Wells Fargo-looking armored trucks and two ambulances.

"Mother! Let me go! Mother!" I yelled and struggled out of her arms. What was this? The trucks slammed to a stop, digging holes in the yard. Humorless-looking men with crew cuts in heroic, wraparound sunglasses and American goatees leaped from the trucks. Fear took me as I saw through the be-vined lattice their weapons flashing in the sunlight.

"Mother, how could you!" I screamed at her, backing up.

"What?"

"What the hell, mommy, you called the cops on me?"

"I did no such thing, Holly. What are you—? Finally, my mother turned around. She saw the trucks and the armed men. "Oh my God!" she yelled. "What the hell is this!?"

"We need to hide," I said to my Android of Ecstasy, but saw that he was already hiding in a bush. Smart. Smart robot. I joined him, hoping the troops hadn't seen me.

But then I saw what was written on the side of the trucks and I was only confused…

The sides of the vehicles read: "Obamacare Neutralization Agency."

Chapter Five

Emerson, Lake and Palmer

"Gayle Williams?" One of the big slabs of beef in a vaguely-looking official outfit said, approaching my mother.

"What the hell is this?" my mother shouted at the man, Tony tagging along behind her looking generally oily and up to no good. "Who are you people? How *dare* you ruin my lawn like this!" Her voice was getting higher and pinched. I'd only heard that voice a few times. I didn't envy the cops.

"Gayle Williams?" the man said again.

"Yes! Yes, you oaf! State your business and state it fast."

"Mother of Holly McQuerty?"

"Again. Yes."

"Do you happen to know where your

daughter is, Mrs. Williams?"

"*Mz.* Williams. And I haven't the faintest."

"I'm sorry to hear that."

"Why are you looking for her?"

"That's classified, ma'am, I'm sorry."

"Oh, *now* he's sorry!" my mother turned to Tony to say.

"Mind if we take a look around your property, ma'am? We have intel the fugitive is in the area. It's for your own safety."

"Actually, yes, I do mind. Take your goon-mobiles and get the hell off my lawn. You can expect a bill for sod repair by the middle of next week."

"Understood," the beef boy said, smiling, but also shaking his head. He turned to one of his 100% all-beef henchmen sporting a very masculine goatee of his own and said something I couldn't hear. The henchman handed the head beef a clipboard from the truck.

"Doctor's orders, ma'am," he said, turning to my mother. "We, acting as agents of the Affordable Care Act Death– um, *Neutralization* Panel, invested with the powers of Obamacare, hereby declare to have authorization to collect you for Emerson, Lake and Palmer."

Silent pause.

"Emerson, Lake and... Who? What?"

"Sorry, an inside joke," he said. "We're all big prog rock fans in the unit. Yes. Gentle Giant. King Crimson. Comus. Marillion. You name it." Some of the agents behind him laughed and shook their heads. "But yeah, E.L.P., I mean."

"E.L.P.?"

The agent wielded a piece of paper from the clipboard. "End of Life Processing."

"This is insane!" my mother yelled, swooning. "What doctor? Who signed this? I'm not sick! I'm the picture of health! Just ask my boy toy, Tony. I can go for *hours!*"

Tony stepped forward as if to speak, but the agent waved him off. "Ma'am, I don't... are you going to come quietly or do we have to use force?"

"Force? *Force!?* This is *my* property. Get off my property *this* instant!"

"Ma'am..."

"Get off my property or I'm calling the police!"

"We *are* the police, lady. The dream police, ha ha."

"No you're not, you fascist scumbags!" my

mother shouted and lifted her keychain, unhooking her pepper spray.

"Gun!" the agent shouted and rolled on the ground.

Another agent stepped forward and tazed my mother. Always with the tazers. She screamed and fell to the grass, shaking violently. Her giant hat flew away like a scared bird. The agent stood over her laughing.

No, no, no!

I couldn't stand it any longer!

"Mumsy!" I screamed. The Obama Sex Robot tried to hold me back, but I popped up from behind the bush. "Leave her alone! It's me! I'm here!" I yelled and ran towards them across the lanai, across the lawn, across destiny.

Two of the goons lifted my mother up by the armpits and threw her in the back of a paddy wagon. Two others apprehended a bewildered, useless, Italian Tony as well and launched him like a sliced-thin, flying piece of prosciutto into the back with her.

"Leave her alone!" I screamed, my belly bouncing as I came across the lawn. "You want me? Well here I am!"

The meat goons swung into action. One beef

pointed his hot dog finger at me, two other sirloin brothers ran at me, handcuffs and tazers at the ready.

Then there was a blur. It was my OSR (Obamacare Sex Robot) Unit passing me. I saw a look of absolute surprise and fear on the face of one of the meat men coming at me. His face quickly changed to one of agony though, as Obama punched him square in the face, smashing his wraparound Oakley's into a million points of light. The beef hit the turf. His twenty-five minute guitar solo-loving, meat compatriot, though, fared better. Tender Beef Two spun around and gave my buddy Obama a roundhouse kick to the dome with his steel-toed boot. Obama's head was titanium—it sounded like a sledgehammer hitting the side of a dumpster. Obama fell over into the grass and the man jumped on him. The two began to roll around on the lawn, wrestling, scratching, snarling. I had a brief vision of a pillow-biting Bradley and Obama on my bed. But that immediately passed... for now the guns came out.

A bullet launched a divot from the grass near my feet like a tee-off from Tiger Woods, Tiger, Tiger Woods, y'all.

I screamed. Two other crew-cutted shanks of loin came at me. Things were looking bad. The jig was up…

But just then another rough 'n tumbled noise of destiny filled the yard…

A car came flying out of nowhere. It was a giant silver truck careening up the driveway towards the lawn at 100 m.p.h.!

People screamed. I know I did. The truck hopped a little speed bump of mulch and roses hemming the driveway and came at us. Some of the Death Agents drew their weapons and fired. Bullets bounced off the grille. Obama and the Beef Man untangled, the beefer kneeling to shoot at the oncoming vehicle.

Still the truck came.

I recognized the truck. Actually, it was an SUV. "Is that—?"

"Yes," The Obamacare Sex Robot said coming up to me, and grabbed my hand, yanking my pregnant butt away from the trajectory of the SUV—*my* SUV—and we ran behind the gazebo.

The engine roared. The bullets flew.

In three nanoseconds the sport utility vehicle with black leather interior reached the center of the lawn and plowed into five of the Death

Agents. Their bodies flew willy-nilly over the hood or crunched under the harum-scarum wheels, their fantastic fascistic fatality screams ringing across the lawn. It was horrible! Horrible! I guess!

Then the SUV did a quick doughnut on the lawn, turned and came at us again. I screamed, ready to die. Unbelievable! *Life… life is what it's all about*, I thought. *Let's keep on doing the living stuff. Martha Stewart Living.* I hugged Obama, waiting for the nasty thud and the darkness.

But the truck swerved at the last second and skidded next to us, its wheels digging holes in the yard. Would the driver be getting a bill for sod repair by the middle of next week as well?

The window rolled down. In the driver's seat was a woman, built like an ATM, mother to Aiden, Jayden and Rayden, a wild and terrible look in her eye, my bitch of a best friend…

"Bethany!?"

"Get in, snizzes!" she screamed.

"I don't understand!" I yelled. In the passenger seat next to her was the albino man from the motel, the one Bethany was beating the shit out of that other guy with. "What's happening? What's…" I started to grow faint.

"No time to explain!" she yelled. A bullet caromed off the bumper.

"But—"

"You can go with the Death Panel or with us! Your choice!"

"But—"

"Hurry!"

Out of the corner of my eye I saw my mother's boy toy Tony whack the distracted agent guarding them in the head. The agent fell to the ground and the two of them jumped out of the Death Panel truck and came running across the grass towards the SUV.

"Okay! Okay!" I shouted.

Everything happened so fast.

My Obama helped me up into the back seat. Then he jumped in behind me. My mother flung the back door open on the other side and leaped inside headfirst screaming as if a scorpion was tweaking her nipples. Tony jumped in and slammed the door.

"Go, bah-a-ah, go!" shouted the furry albino riding shotgun, all tittery, jittery, wild-eyed and weird.

Bethany slammed on the gas and we escaped towards the driveway over the green grass, bullets ricocheting off the back of the SUV, sunny blue skies and heavenly, Caucasian clouds over Connecticut…

CHAPTER SIX
Totally Plez-Botting

Bethany's arm disappeared inside my Sex Robot's ass up to her elbow. "This should take just a second," she said, smiling.

I'd known Bethany my entire life. We were in the same kindergarten class together, Mrs. Barrington's. Her house was only three streets from mine growing up, and we became fast frenemies. She excelled at using the rules of society as a weapon—a prodigy really. When we were six she drew pictures of Barbie and Jem with crayons all over her dining room wall. When her mother came in and saw it, Bethany blamed it on me. Sort of. She actually told me to admit to it. 'Say you did it *on purpose*,' Little Bethany whispered in my ear, and, not knowing what 'on purpose' meant but thinking it regal and adult, I repeated the words to her mother. This was the first time I'd been 'in trouble' with another parent. It was strange and frightening—her mother was an imposing, huge lady with a lion's mane of hair and a booming voice (and this DNA was passed to her offspring, most noticeably her thick brown hair). To who or what strange gods were these other parents accountable? A kid never knew. With fear beating against the cage of my heart like a little bird I was locked in a dark linen closet for what seemed like a thousand years until their maid Eustace accidentally rescued me (possibly on purpose, I suppose now as I think back on it). A week later Bethany apologized to me with a handful of chocolates and I accepted her apology. And when she apologized for having given me chocolates that were in fact from a box of laxatives stolen from her parents' medicine cabinet as an apology I accepted that apology as well a week (spent unpleasantly) later. In high school she keyed the car of Graham Creighton-Simms, a boyfriend who broke my heart and dumped me two weeks before the Junior Prom for blonde-miss-thing-with-tig-ol'-bitties Jessica Tufte. Jessica Tufte fared only slightly better: "*Slut Bitch*" appeared spray-painted on her locker the next Monday morning and—I suppose this was somewhat worse—fell down the flight of stairs behind the science wing under mysterious circumstances on Tuesday, breaking a leg and bittie-supporting rib.

At Yale, Bethany had a string of boyfriends and even a couple girlfriends, giving the L.U.G. thing the old college try. But by the time she'd graduated she'd hooked the man of her dreams—that is, a boy rich enough to support her so she didn't have to work: Graham Creighton-Simms. Yes, *that* Graham Creighton-Simms, who had also gone to Yale. By expert flirtation and nefarious blue-balling she managed to twine young master Graham around her finger, his head a mess of cum-crusted desires, until he had no recourse but to propose. Had it been her plan all along, I wondered, since the keying-of-his-car incident in High School? Their wedding was the W.A.S.P. "Event of the Season" in affluent Connecticut. She, the robust, boisterous daughter of an Aetna VP, he the son of the wealthy owner of the exclusive country club everyone we knew of means and inclination frequented. During the wedding reception at the very same country club, Bethany vomited cake and about fifty Long

Island Iced Teas on the bassist of the wedding band she was jerking off in a broom closet. They had three beautiful children, Aiden, Jayden and Rayden. As a wedding gift for me and Bradley, four years later, Bethany and Graham bought us a shiny new Lexus SUV, the very same smashed and shot-up SUV now parked behind a vacant strip mall, a highly- very- super- totally- motley group of people standing around watching her fist anally the robotic *Gratification System* version of the President of the United States that had been mailed to me for what purposes I would never understand. Yes, I'd known Bethany my entire life, but suddenly it seemed that I didn't know her at all...

"Hold still, Obama Hussein, will you?" Bethany said, gripping a sumptuously crafted butt cheek.

"It is uncomfortable, the action you are performing," The Obamacare Sex Robot said. There were squishing noises. Electric zapping. I plugged my ears but could not look away. My robot companion was pantsless, legs spread, his arms across the hood of the SUV as if he were being arrested and molested.

"You can feel that?" Bethany said.

"Yes," Obama replied.

"You feel pain?"

A grunt. "Yes."

"Must be new *avec les* latest mods." She turned to her muscly albino escort and pinched his chiseled and cottony thigh with her free hand.

"Ouch!" he bleated after a brief moment of cogitation, then hopped around on one leg.

"Cool!" Bethany said and resumed her butt-work. My *Bx-44* squirmed, his legs shook on the pavement. I felt sorry for him, but I was not as sorry as I was confused at what was happening, of why we were doing this.

After Bethany's daring rescue the speeding car was chaos incarnate: My mother a flooding brook of babbling and teary nonsense; Tony unsuccessfully attempting to comfort her in his Italian arms like a warm bun cradling a tender veal parm; the strange white man bleating and baaing directions to Bethany from the front passenger seat; Obama rubbing my tummy, trying to finger me through my dress; my hyperventilating; my swatting away Obama's fingers; Bethany singing along very loudly to Alanis Morissette blaring on the stereo.

"But won't they be looking for a silver SUV

now!? How the hell'd you find my car!?" I sat forward in the speeding car and screamed into Bethany's ear.

Bethany finished a chorus out and then turned down the music. "No, well, yes," she said. "They *were* looking for a stolen red Datsun, but yeah, since I rescued your asses they'll be looking for this beat up POS SUV again. That's why we're gonna ditch it and get back into mine. Duh. I knew we'd be seen at your mother's house, but I didn't think the D.P.'s'd be there *already*. Those fucking bitches are getting faster. Wising up. So the main thing... we really gotta get your plez-bot's node out, like, *yesterday*."

"Node?"

"GPS node, snizz-face!"

Bethany had then swerved into (yet another— Thanks Obama) abandoned strip mall and shot around to the back. We all piled out and she commanded that the Commander in Chief take his pants off and bend over the hood. Strangely, he obeyed.

"Wait! Wait... I think I... hold on... Yup... there... wait, wait... ooh, this one is *way* different... hold on, there, no, yes! Wait... okay... hold on... wait, yup, there it is, okay...

wait, wait, wait… hold on, yes, ooh, weird, it's like, new, okay, hold on, no, no… just a sec, s'really, really tight up here… no, there it is, this guy's a giver not a taker that is obvious to—hold on—me, I can feel it riiiiiiiight there… shit, fuck, okay, so tight, tighter than a breadbox, hold on, tight is mighty right, wait, wait, just a second, this is so… weird… it's like it's—okay, okay, got it! I think… yes! Got it! Got it, you magnificent son of a snizz!" Bethany said.

She did one final strange maneuver up inside the imposter's posterior and then yanked out a piece of electronic equipment from between his quivery cheeks—what looked like a computer chip with wires hanging off it. Some cheap ham radio chunk of electronics from Radio Shack.

"Bethany, you're a mother-scratching genius!" Bethany said, standing. She held the thing up for all of us to see and then chucked it into the woods. Then, one by one, she took our phones from us and smashed them on the pavement. "Aight, let's 5000, snizzles!"

"But what ab—"

"In the car!" she yelled.

Only more confused, we piled into Bethany's black Escalade, she put a CD in the stereo and we jetted off down the road, "You Oughta Know" blasting at such ear-splitting volume I was worried it would deafen my unborn child.

I made it all the way to the part where Alanis sings about sucking Dave Coulier's dick in a movie theater before confusion and rage swamped my senses.

"GODDAMMITBETHANYWHATTHEFU CKISGOINGONWHYISEVERYONETRYIN GTOKILLUSNOWANDWHOTHEFUCKIST HISALBINOWEIRDO!?!?!?!?!?!?" I screamed over Alanis.

The Escalade swerved, nearly driving into an oncoming truck. Bethany threw up her hands, screaming. The jerking motion made the CD skip and then finally stop. The screaming in the car that replaced the music might actually have been louder than the music. The oncoming truck's aggrieved horn was blasting at us, its grill grimacing in our eyeballs.

At the last second the weirdo white dude grabbed the steering wheel and flung us back into our lane. (Ain't that always the way?)

"Leroy, you're a life saver," Bethany said to the guy.

It took a second for that to sink in.

"Leroy?" my mom queried.

"Leroy… *the Lamb?*" I said.

"Yup!" Bethany laughed.

Leroy the Lamb-Man joined in with his own weird little titterous bleat of a laughing animal guffaw attempt. Happy to be included, but also obviously confused and scared and out of place and knowing it.

"How the hell, is… what? I'm so…" I trailed off, sitting back in my seat.

"Look, I'll spare you the suspense," Bethany said, eyes on the road, hands at 10 and 2. "He's my Obamacare Sex Robot, okay? The night of your baby shower I went home and went online. I was *suuuper* fucking 'faced. *You* remember. And Graham and I had a huge fight, natch', when he picked me up. I'm a little hazy on the deets myself, but I pieced it together like a boss, like Inspector Effing Clouseau. When we got home, Graham went to bed and I went online. There were two windows open the next day. One was the Lamb Rental Farm website and one was Healthcare.gov. You getting a bot delivered made me want one—sorry. But I was also *soooo* in love with Leroy. I wanted to check out his site, maybe buy him off the farm. Silly me… I think I might have mixed up windows by accident on purpose on accident. In the place on the form for what you want your plez-bot to look like I must have uploaded a picture of Leroy. And voila! The next day Leroy shows up in a box. Total cute-ass sexy-ass furry-ass Leroy. I'd spent the extra $37,000 for expedited processing. Of course, Graham was suuuuper pissed. He was all like, *Dammit Beth, you already have ten goddamned Obamacare Sex Robots*, and I was like, *So do you*, and he was all, *I never loved you*, and then I laughed and was like, *There is literally no one else on this Earth who would ever touch your hairy, gross balls, and that includes that fucking slut Jessica Tufte you cock-muncher, so you're stuck with me*, but then he was like, *Holy shit, have you seen the news today? Your friend Holly assaulted a police officer.* And the rest is history, so that's that."

"But I don't get it. How did you find us at the motel? We were fifty miles from town." I said.

"Oh, we at the club have our ways," Bethany said.

"But what about—"

"Jesus! Can you just wait until we get there?"

"Where!? *Where* are you taking us?" I said.

"The safest place on earth for people like us."

"Like who?" my mother asked.

"Three women and three robots. We're like the Six Musketeers! We should *totally* have a six-way when we get there! That was be *awss.*"

"Get where?" I said again, assuming (correctly) that I would not be answered this crucial question, as I was an outlaw and fugitive from justice.

"Don't you mean three women, two robots and a *man?*" my mother quavered next to me.

Bethany laughed and kept driving, as if my mother had quipped deliciously a tasty witticism into the conversation. The green trees of Connecticut blurred past like silent and stupid square-celled witnesses to history. But then Bethany's laugh petered out, and she turned around to look wide-eyed at my mother, as if gauging my mother's sincerity—her whole shit.

"Wait, you mean you *don't* know?" Bethany said. "Oh my God, of *course* you don't. Gayle... Oily Tony's an Affordable Care Act Sex Robot too. You've totally been plez-botting this whole time! Gayle, *all* the caddy-gigolos at the Country Club are plez-bots. Duh!"

CHAPTER SEVEN
Wary of the Cray-Cray

The rest of the trip was spent in stony, watery, fiery silence.

My mother could not be induced to speak. She was suffering from insult-induced shock (a normal enough occurrence with people of our milky social ilk). Though greasy Tony's roaming hands rushed and rushing fingers roamed, his offer of a massage was repeatedly rejected by Mumsy. One after another scary cray-cray armored vehicle passed us on the road, as if the whole state of Connecticut were kitting up for a race war. I sat thinking nervously behind Bethany (those mental racquetballs getting another serious workout); there was way too much new data to parse, way TMI. And it seemed that at any minute one of these behemoths would turn its turret to us and blow us to Kingdom Cum, which did not in any way aid in concentration.

We came to the Club, the one Bethany's husband had inherited from his rich daddy when he died, the very same one my mother went to, and apparently the one all the old ladies in the tri-county area patronized to get their "plezzing" freak on, and drove in through the swirly-ornate, metal front entrance probably blacksmithed by a Mayflower passenger.

"What the fuck," I said, snapping out of racquetball central. "Why here?"

"It's safe, Hol'," Bethany said.

She turned off the main drive onto an access road I'd never seen or noticed before. Soon we came to a heavy green gate. It opened automatically. On the other side of the gate, the woods were thick, old growth, nowhere near as manicured as the rest of the club, which (I thought) was mostly a golf course. We drove for another twenty minutes. The gravel road went up and winded around a steep hill. I realized Obama's hand was resting on my breast and had been rubbing my nipple without me knowing it. A heat between my legs informed me it must have been a while. I blushed. And hoped nobody else saw.

"How the hell big is this place anyway? I've never seen these woods," I said, knocking Obama's hand away.

"Oh, whose woods these are I think I know..." Bethany intoned.

Her Obamacare Sex Robot Man-Sheep baaed a laugh, said, "His house is in the village though." Apparently this unit had come with a poetry CD-ROM, as well as a soft, fleecy coat of wool. Seriously, dude was like a white Chewbacca. With a six-pack, hard muscles and cute dimples appointing his handsome, yet ovine face, with its small black eyes and pointy pink ears. "And miles to go before I sheep / and miles to go before I sheep!" He and Bethany shared a laugh. I shook my head. Obama tweaked a nip. Oily Tony ran a hand along my mother's thigh. My mother batted it away, a tear on her cheek.

"Boom," said Bethany.

The Escalade rounded a bend and the road ended abruptly. A cliff of gray stone rose up a hundred feet from the forest floor. Bethany accelerated towards it and—for what seemed like the millionth time that road trip—the inside of the car erupted into screams, bleats and flailing limbs.

Bethany accelerated the SUV to suicide speed. Obama wrapped his arms around my stomach. Tony cupped my mother's breasts like real *polpette con sentimento*. Leroy began frantically tweaking his own nipples, his leg bouncing up and down like a jackhammer.

Then Bethany touched what looked like a garage door opener on her sun visor and the stone began to move. "Open plez-a-me!" she yelled. The stone opened like a double French door and we flew through the wall.

We drove through and I was fully expecting us to plunge down into some Bat Cave or underground tunnel, but there was only more woods, same as before. The gravel road continued as it had been, between towering deciduous and evergreens.

After another fifteen minutes we reached our destination. However many miles later we came to an ornate, old mansion, five stories high with a mansard roof, covered in ivy. It looked like a boarding school out of a 19th century English novel—some place where young boys were tormented by upper classmen and spanked with paddles between Latin lessons. A very specific type of Eden.

Bethany pulled the Escalade to a stop and got out. Leroy scampered from the truck and hippity-hopped after her but the rest of us stayed inside, wary of everything. Wary of the cray-cray.

Presently, the front door to the mansion swung open and an old man in a blue bathrobe and slippers came out, smiling, arms spread wide. Bethany ran to him and they hugged. We could hear their muffled talk through the windshield.

"You made it!" The man said. He had a thin, intelligent face, the untroubled face of a rich older man free from worry, and a full head of white hair. "I'm *so* glad. Everyone will be *so* happy." And the man looked over Bethany's shoulder at the SUV. "So… this is her? This is the one you told me about," he said.

Inside the car my mother said, "Where have I seen that man before? I know I've seen him somewhere. That hair…"

Outside, Bethany let go of the man and turned. "Oh, hells yes. Wasn't no thang. Just a few Deep-derps at her mother's. We kicked 'em to the curb and GTF outta there!"

"Good, good, good. And were you followed?"

"Not a chance."

"Good, good, good."

"Phones?"

"Smashed."

"Good, good, good."

Bethany pumped a big arm at the car for us to come out.

"Well, we're here now," I lamented.

"Wherever *here* is," my mother replied. "But is that…?"

We got out and our Obamacare Sex Robots, Tony and Obama, followed.

Bethany did the introductions. "Harrison Creighton-Simms, this is everyone. Everyone, this is Mr. Harrison Creighton-Simms. He's our leader here. Graham's father, only the ninth director of the Country Club's storied three hundred years."

My mother gasped.

"Um, Bethany…" I said.

"Yeah?"

I inhaled as much air as I possibly could and then, raising my head up to the trees and scrunching my body as tight as it would go, screamed at the top of my lungs: "WHERETHEFUCKISFUCKINGHEREYOU FUCKINGBIIIIIIIIIIIIIIIIIIIIIIIIIIIIIIIIIIIIIIIIIIII IIIIIIIIIIIIIIIIIIIIIIIIIIIIIIIIIIIIIIIIIIIIIIITCH!!!!!!!

???????"

Sparklers and color-wads popped and wobbled in my eyes. My throat went hot and hoarse, my legs jellified and my Obama Man-Bot with a whir of gears and computer code grabbed me by the arms and held me up before I puddled on the ground.

I caught my breath. I righted myself. When I came to, Harrison Creighton-Simms was laughing. "I see Bethany has gone classic Bethany on you," he said, "Typical suburban sweetheart jibber-jabber and nonsense with zero explanation whatsoever."

"Guilty," Bethany laughed.

"But our *very best* soldier," the old man said. "Do come inside. Do, and everything will be explained. With refreshments. Wonderful!"

The man clapped like a sheik.

A handful of pretty young males and females in flowing togas hastened from the mansion and ushered us inside…

Dear Reader,

As a purveyor of the written word, I survive on interaction with my readers. If you have the time and enjoyed any part of what you just read, please review this book anywhere you see fit: Amazon, Goodreads, twitter, whatever!

It's the 90's now... Reviews and word of mouth on the internet are truly the life's blood of any writer. And I love hearing from readers. So tell me what you think!

Thanks again and happy reading,
xoxo
Lacey

ABOUT THE AUTHOR

Well, let me tell you about good ol' Lacey Noonan. Lacey lives on the east coast with her family. When not sailing, sampling fine whiskeys or making veggie tacos, she loves to read and write steamy, strange, silly, psychological and sexy stories. During daylight hours she is a web designer and developer, but mostly a mom.

For more information on Lacey Noonan, why not point your browser snake at:

Amazon Author Profile
amazon.com/author/laceynoonan

Mailing List
http://eepurl.com/bEeNgv

Facebook
facebook.com/laceynoonan123

Twitter
twitter.com/laceynoonan

Email
laceynoonan123@gmail.com

OTHER BOOKS BY *Lacey Noonan*

SEDUCED BY THE DAD BOD: BOOK ONE IN THE CHILL DAD SUMMER HEAT SERIES

Amanda's back from college for the summer, sexy and bored. Mr. Baldwin is a chill dad who loves swimming, singing '90s hits, Super Soakers and has a body like a big sack of wet sugar. What happens when these two star-crossed lovers cross paths? And oh yeah—he's her boyfriend's dad? Uh-oh! By turns devastatingly erotic and incisive, this first installment of Lacey Noonan's hot new summery Dad Bod saga will leave you questioning everything in your life.

HOT BOXED: HOW I FOUND LOVE ON AMAZON

Hot Boxed is the story of Randi, a 20-something girl working at an Amazon Distribution Center who wants more out of life. Assuming she'll work there forever, a name pops up on her scanner that ignites her passions. Does she have the courage to break the chains that bind her, to step out of her dreary life and do something so, so, so crazy to get what she wants? Find out in this super-steamy story!

I Don't Care if My Best Friend's Mom is a Sasquatch, She's Hot and I'm Taking a Shower With Her… Because It's the New Millennium

Life for Jason is one wild experience after another. But then one night, a chance encounter dredges up a long-forgotten mystery, and suddenly he is trapped on a roller coaster of wildness. Is it more wildness than he can handle? Now he is on the run with his star-crossed lover. Will they reach a shower in time, or will the natural heat that burns within her consume them both? Literally, the steamiest book you will read all year!

I Don't Care If My Sasquatch Lover Says the World is Exploding, She's Hot But I Play Bass and There's Nothing Hotter Right Now Than Rap-Rock
(…Because It's the New Millennium • Book Two)

Star-crossed lovers Jason and Starla are back in this devastatingly sexy and fun sequel. On the run from the devious Lemaire family and lost in the woods for weeks looking for the rendezvous that will get them to Starla's homeland, they are at their wits end when Jason abruptly joins the rap-rock band 311 (currently on tour with the Lilith Fair), throwing their whirlwind romance—and their very lives—into jeopardy. Welcome to the new millennium! Or is it?

THE BABYSITTER ONLY RINGS ONCE

This is NOT your typical babysitter story... One night when Sophie realizes she's left something scandalous at the Lindstrom's—the affluent family she has babysat for years now—she goes against all the fibers of her being and decides to get it back—no matter what, even if it means more scandal. Find out what Sophie recovers in this seriously HOT and suspenseful story by Lacey Noonan.

EAT FRESH: FLO, JAN & WENDY AND THE FIVE DOLLAR FOOTLONG

"God damn, marketing events are bitch." And so begins the sexy, wild adventures of our three protagonists, Jan, Flo and Wendy—the three hottest stars of the contemporary TV commercial scene. After a fight with Wendy's agent, the girls take it upstairs to Flo's VIP hotel room, where they soon discover the pleasures of each other's bodies—as well as the very valuable, last remaining Five Dollar Footlong at the event. Caution: Hottt!

A GRONKING TO REMEMBER:
BOOK ONE IN THE ROB GRONKOWSKI EROTICA SERIES

Leigh has a serious problem. And it's driving a "spike" between her and her husband Dan. When she accidentally witnesses the NFL's biggest wrecking ball, Rob Gronkowski of the New England Patriots, do his patented "Gronk Spike," she is suddenly hornier than she's ever been. This causes her to go on a rampage of her own—a rampage of "self-discovery." And soon everyone's lives have changed. Romance! Sports!

A GRONKING TO REMEMBER 2: CHAD GOES DEEP IN THE NEUTRAL ZONE (BOOK TWO IN THE ROB GRONKOWSKI EROTICA SERIES)

The saga continues! When Leigh spurns his advances at a party he throws in her honor, Dan's friend Chad kidnaps her, stealing her away to his personal New England Patriots Shangri-La, a secret Man Cave hundreds of feet below sea level he affectionately calls his "Chadmiral's Quarters." There she learns about a side of Gronk she'd never known, changing her life forever. Secrets will be revealed—Gronktastic secrets. Possibly the greatest sequel ever written. Makes the original look like a certified *piece of shit!*

A CRUZMAS CAROL: TED CRUZ TAKES A DICKENS OF A CONSTITUTIONAL

Ted Cruz is *done* with politics. He's throwing himself a sex-fueled, drunken bacchanal and then he's joining the private sector. But his plans are about to change. After a hot makeout sesh with his sexy staffer Roberta, Ted has a digestive emergency and sprints to the men's room, where he runs into an old, long-dead coworker. Irritated, not heeding this magical spirit's warnings, Ted is told he will be visited by three more ghosts before the night is over. And so within minutes Ted is being sucked through glory hole after ol' glory hole to the past, present and future to learn some heartwarming lessons about America, freedom and also American freedom.

SHIPWRECKED ON THE ISLAND OF THE SHE-GODS: A SOUTH PACIFIC TRANS SEX ADVENTURE

Shipwrecked on the Island of the She-Gods is a seriously sexually-charged adventure of heart-pounding exotica that doesn't skimp on story or skimpily-clad native girls with "a little something extra." And it's a little something extra that Noah, Julian and Owen will experience over and over in the steamy jungle, along the shores and atop towering mountains until they're begging for mercy. And then begging for more.

THE HOTNESS: FIVE
BURNING HOT NOVELLAS

PREPARE TO BE TURNED THE HELL ON. Here are five novellas that will titillate and drive you wild, running the gamut of erotic fantasies. If you've ever wanted all of Lacey Noonan's books in one easy, accessible place for one low price, then this is the book for you, sexy-pants. Contains the novellas: *Submitting the Landlord; Hot Boxed: How I Found Love on Amazon; The Babysitter Only Rings Once; I Don't Care if My Best Friend's Mom is a Sasquatch, She's Hot and I'm Taking a Shower With Her (...Because It's the New Millennium);* and *Eat Fresh: Flo, Jan & Wendy and the Five Dollar Footlong.*

THE NASTY WOMAN'S GUIDE TO
DEPLORABLE BASKETS

Here is the most comprehensive book on baskets ever published. Guiding you on your baskety journey are the Ladies of the New England Basket Weavers Association. An energetic bunch, they are as varied as the baskets they weave. Some weave as a hobby. Some weave to put food on the table. Some are old. Some are young. But all of them are complete bitches. It's up to you to decide who is who and who will survive the inevitable grudge-match and battle of egos which will more than likely tear the fabric of the club apart like a pack of nasty wolves. So hop aboard the Basket Train. Next stop: Baskets! As Madge Beaverworth says in her wonderful introduction: "Baskets, baskets, baskets!"

Made in the USA
Las Vegas, NV
01 November 2023